lots of
knock-
knock
jokes
for
kids

lots of knock-knock jokes for kids

By Whee Winn

ZONDERKIDZ

Lots of Knock-Knock Jokes for Kids
Copyright © 2016 by Zonderkidz

This title is also available as a Zondervan ebook.
Visit www.zondervan.com/ebooks.

Requests for information should be addressed to:
Zonderkidz, 3900 Sparks Dr. SE, Grand Rapids, Michigan 49546

ISBN 978-0-310-75062-8

Cover design: *Brand Navigation*
Interior design: *Denise Froehlich*

Printed in China

18 19 20 21 22 23 /DSC/ 10 9 8 7 6 5 4 3 2 1

Note to Jokesters

Knock-knock jokes are pretty common.

Lots of people tell them—kids and adults. Some are pretty funny. Some are very corny. Others make no sense at all. But no matter what your opinion of knock-knock jokes is, one thing most people can agree on is that kids love them!! And I hope you are one of those kids because . . .

. . . if you are looking for funny, corny, crazy knock-knock jokes this is the book for you!

Lots of Knock-Knock Jokes for Kids is an awesome collection of good, clean, corny jokes that will make you roll your eyes, snort, giggle, groan, and laugh til you cry.

Knock, knock.
Who's there?
Olive.
Olive who?
Olive a good joke! Do you?

Table of Contents

Table of Contents:

1

Name Jokes

Knock, knock.
Who's there?
Harry.
Harry who?
Harry up, it's cold out here!

Knock, knock.
Who's there?
William.
William who?
William mind your own business!

Knock, knock.
Who's there?
Noah.
Noah who?
Noah good place we can get something to eat?

Knock, knock.
Who's there?
Dora.
Dora who?
Dora's locked. That's why I'm knocking!

Knock, knock.
Who's there?
Howard.
Howard who?
Howard you?

Knock, knock.
Who's there?
Phillip.
Phillip who?
Phillip your pool. I wanna take a dip!

Knock, knock.
Who's there?
Jo.
Jo who?
Jo King!

Knock, knock.
Who's there?
Iva.
Iva who?
Iva sore hand from knocking.

Knock, knock.
Who's there?
Anita.
Anita who?
Anita borrow a pencil.

Knock, knock.
Who's there?
Dwayne.
Dwayne who?
Dwayne the bathtub, it's overflowing!

Knock, knock.
Who's there?
Lena.
Lena who?
Lena little closer and I'll tell you.

Knock, knock.
Who's there?
Mikey.
Mikey who?
Mikey doesn't fit in the hole!

Knock, knock.
Who's there?
Kent.
Kent who?
Kent you tell by my voice?

Knock, knock.
Who's there?
Luke.
Luke who?
Luke through the peephole and find out!

Knock, knock.
Who's there?
Jess.
Jess who?
Jess me and my shadow!

Knock, knock.
Who's there?
Arfur.
Arfur who?
Arfur got!

Knock, knock.
Who's there?
Isabel.
Isabel who?
Isabel working? I had to knock!

Knock, knock.
Who's there?
Barbie.
Barbie who?
Barbie Q. Chicken!

Knock, knock.
Who's there?
Nana.
Nana who?
Nana your business!

Knock, knock.
Who's there?
Amy.
Amy who?
Amy 'fraid I've forgotten.

Knock, knock.
Who's there?
Justin.
Justin who?
Justin the neighborhood, thought I would drop by.

Knock, knock.
Who's there?
Ben.
Ben who?
Ben knocking for ten minutes!

Knock, knock.
Who's there?
Emma.
Emma who?
Emma bit cold out here, could you let me in?

Knock, knock.
Who's there?
Maya.
Maya who?
Maya name is Dan.

Knock, knock.
Who's there?
Dewey.
Dewey who?
Dewey have to keep telling silly jokes?

Knock, knock.
Who's there?
Mary Lee.
Mary Lee who?
Mary Lee, Mary Lee, Mary Lee, Mary Lee, life is but a dream!

Knock, knock.
Who's there?
Abe.
Abe who?
Abe C D E F G . . .

Knock, knock.
Who's there?
Alex.
Alex who?
Alex-plain later!

Knock, knock.
Who's there?
Ivana.
Ivana who?
Ivana come in!

Knock, knock.
Who's there?
Carl.
Carl who?
Carl get you there faster than a bike!

Knock, knock.
Who's there?
Norma Lee.
Norma Lee who?
Norma Lee I don't go around knocking on doors, but I just had to meet you!

Knock, knock.
Who's there?
Oswald.
Oswald who?
Oswald my bubblegum.

Knock, knock.
Who's there?
Adam.
Adam who?
Adam my way, I'm coming through!

Knock, knock.
Who's there?
Olive.
Olive who?
Olive right next door.

Knock, knock.
Who's there?
Otto.
Otto who?
Otto know. I've got amnesia.

Knock, knock.
Who's there?
Scott.
Scott who?
Scott nothing to do with you!

Knock, knock.
Who's there?
Ida.
Ida who?
Ida like to be your friend!

Knock, knock.
Who's there?
Howard.
Howard who?
Howard you know unless you open the door?

Knock, knock.
Who's there?
Wanda.
Wanda who?
Wanda buy some Girl Scout cookies?

Knock, knock.
Who's there?
Doris.
Doris who?
Doris locked, that's why I knocked!

Knock, knock.
Who's there?
Mae.
Mae who?
Mae be I'll tell you and Mae be I won't!

Knock, knock.
Who's there?
Sabina.
Sabina who?
Sabina long time since I've seen you!

Knock, knock.
Who's there?
Sacha.
Sacha who?
Sacha lot of questions.

Knock, knock.
Who's there?
Brad.
Brad who?
I've got Brad news, I'm afraid!

Knock, knock.
Who's there?
Abbott.
Abbott who?
Abbott time you opened this door!

Knock, knock.
Who's there?
Frank.
Frank who?
Frank you for being my friend.

Knock, knock.
Who's there?
Isaiah.
Isaiah who?
Isaiah nothing until you open this door!

Knock, knock.
Who's there?
Ali.
Ali who?
Ali wanna do is have some fun.

Knock, knock.
Who's there?
Shelby.
Shelby who?
Shelby coming around the mountain when she comes. Shelby coming around the mountain when she comes. Shelby coming around the mountain. Shelby coming around the mountain. Shelby coming around the mountain when she comes!

Knock, knock.
Who's there?
Dawn.
Dawn who?
Dawn leave me out in the cold!

Knock, knock.
Who's there?
Omar.
Omar who?
Omar goodness! This is the wrong door!

Knock, knock.
Who's there?
Alma.
Alma who?
Alma not going to tell you.

Knock, knock.
Who's there?
Avery.
Avery who?
Avery time I come to your house we go through this again!

Knock, knock.
Who's there?
Sam.
Sam who?
Sam day you'll recognize me.

Knock, knock.
Who's there?
Sara.
Sara who?
Sara 'nother way in?

Knock, knock.
Who's there?
Elias.
Oh, hi, Elias, come in, come in.
You're supposed to say, "Elias who?"

Knock, knock.
Who's there?
Harry.
Harry who?
Harry up and you will find out!

Knock, knock.
Who's there?
Shirley.
Shirley who?
Shirley you must know me by now!

Knock, knock.
Who's there?
Benny.
Benny who?
Benny thing happening with you today?

Knock, knock.
Who's there?
Al.
Al who?
Al give you a hug if you let me in!

Knock, knock.
Who's there?
Simon.
Simon who?
Simon the other side of the door. If you opened up, you'd see!

Knock, knock.
Who's there?
Juno.
Juno who?
Juno who it is!

Knock, knock.
Who's there?
Sloane.
Sloane who?
Sloanely outside. Let me in!

Knock, knock.
Who's there?
Theodore.
Theodore who?
Theodore was locked so I knocked!

Knock, knock.
Who's there?
Abbey.
Abbey who?
Abbey stung me on the nose!

Knock, knock.
Who's there?
Manuel.
Manuel who?
Manuel be sorry if you don't answer this door!

Knock, knock.
Who's there?
Isaiah.
Isaiah who?
Isaiah 'gain, knock, knock!

Knock, knock.
Who's there?
Annie.
Annie who?
Annie body home?

Knock, knock.
Who's there?
Barry.
Barry who?
Barry nice to see you!

Knock, knock.
Who's there?
Pete.
Pete who?
Pete-za delivery!

Knock, knock.
Who's there?
Marie.
Marie who?
Marie me? I love you!

Knock, knock.
Who's there?
Ewan.
Ewan who?
No, it's just me!

Knock, knock.
Who's there?
Danielle.
Danielle who?
Danielle so loud! I heard you the first time!

Knock, knock.
Who's there?
Althea.
Althea who?
Althea later alligator!

Knock, knock.
Who's there?
Denise.
Denise who?
Denise are above the ankles.

Knock, knock.
Who's there?
Maura.
Maura who?
Maura the merrier!

Knock, knock.
Who's there?
Rita.
Rita who?
Rita book, you might learn something!

Knock, knock.
Who's there?
Justin.
Justin who?
Justin time for dinner!

Knock, knock.
Who's there?
Max.
Max who?
Max no difference!

Knock, knock.
Who's there?
Ivan.
Ivan who?
Ivan idea you know who it is!

Knock, knock.
Who's there?
Uriah.
Uriah who?
Keep uriah on the ball!

Knock, knock.
Who's there?
Hal.
Hal who?
Halloo to you too!

Knock, knock.
Who's there?
Meg.
Meg who?
**Meg up your mind! Are you going
to let me in or not?**

Knock, knock.
Who's there?
Haman.
Haman who?
Haman! It's cold out here!

Knock, knock.
Who's there?
Mia.
Mia who?
Mia and my shadow!

Knock, knock.
Who's there?
Gladys.
Gladys who?
Gladys the weekend, aren't you?

Knock, knock.
Who's there?
Greta.
Greta who?
You Greta on my nerves!

Knock, knock.
Who's there?
Mickey.
Mickey who?
Mickey is lost! That's why I'm knocking!

Knock, knock.
Who's there?
Howard.
Howard who?
Howard can it be to guess a knock-knock joke?

Knock, knock.
Who's there?
Mischa.
Mischa who?
I Mischa a lot!

Knock, knock.
Who's there?
Les.
Les who?
Les go out and play.

Knock, knock.
Who's there?
Luke.
Luke who?
Luke through the peephole and find out.

Knock, knock.
Who's there?
Ida.
Ida who?
Ida know. Sorry!

Knock, knock.
Who's there?
Linda.
Linda who?
Linda hand! I can't do it all by myself!

Knock, knock.
Who's there?
Ken.
Ken who?
Ken you open the door and let me in?

Knock, knock.
Who's there?
Cain.
Cain who?
Cain I come in, please?

Knock, knock.
Who's there?
Owen.
Owen who?
Owen are you going to let me in?

Knock, knock.
Who's there?
Nadia.
Nadia who?
Nadia head if you understand me.

Knock, knock.
Who's there?
Stan.
Stan who?
Stan back! I'm knocking this door down!

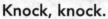

Knock, knock.
Who's there?
Juan.
Juan who?
**Juan to hear some more of these
knock knock jokes?**

2

Place Jokes

Knock, knock.
Who's there?
Utah.
Utah who?
Utah-king to me?

Knock, knock.
Who's there?
Europe.
Europe who?
Europe to no good!

Knock, knock.
Who's there?
Ohio.
Ohio who?
Oh, hi, how are you doing?

Knock, knock.
Who's there?
Venice.
Venice who?
Venice your mother coming home?

Knock, knock.
Who's there?
Babylon.
Babylon who?
Babylon. I'm not really listening.

Knock, knock.
Who's there?
Russian.
Russian who?
Stop Russian me!

Knock, knock.
Who's there?
Alaska.
Alaska who?
Alaska 'nother person if you don't know the answer.

Knock, knock.
Who's there?
Guinea.
Guinea who?
Guinea high five!

Knock, knock.
Who's there?
Avenue.
Avenue who?
Avenue heard this joke before?

Knock, knock.
Who's there?
Indonesia.
Indonesia who?
I see you and I get weak Indonesia!

Knock, knock.
Who's there?
Sodom.
Sodom who?
Sodom earlier, but didn't talk to them.

Knock, knock.
Who's there?
Norway.
Norway who?
Norway will I leave until you open this door!

Knock, knock.
Who's there?
Iran.
Iran who?
Iran all the way over here to tell you something.

Knock, knock.
Who's there?
Area.
Area who?
Area there? It's me!

Knock, knock.
Who's there?
Jamaica.
Jamaica who?
Jamaica great friend!

Knock, knock.
Who's there?
Chile.
Chile who?
It's getting Chile out here, let me in!

Knock, knock.
Who's there?
Uruguay.
Uruguay who?
You go Uruguay and I'll go mine!

Knock, knock.
Who's there?
Heaven.
Heaven who?
Heaven seen you in a while.

Knock, knock.
Who's there?
Germany.
Germany who?
Germany people knock on your door?

Knock, knock.
Who's there?
Aisle.
Aisle who?
Aisle see you around!

Knock, knock.
Who's there?
Juneau.
Juneau who?
Juneau what time it is?

Knock, knock.
Who's there?
Kenya.
Kenya who?
**Kenya keep the noise down?
I'm trying to sleep!**

3

Holiday Jokes

Knock, knock.
Who's there?
Twig.
Twig who?
Twig or tweat!

Knock, knock.
Who's there?
Murray.
Murray who?
Murray Christmas to all and to all a good night!

Knock, knock.
Who's there?
Snow.
Snow who?
Snow one is gonna open the door.

Knock, knock.
Who's there?
Witch.
Witch who?
Witch one of you can fix my broomstick?

Knock, knock.
Who's there?
Sherwood.
Sherwood who?
Sherwood like to be your Valentine!

Knock, knock.
Who's there?
Adore.
Adore who?
Adore is between us. Open up!

Knock, knock.
Who's there?
Osborn.
Osborn who?
Osborn today—it's my birthday!

Knock, knock.
Who's there?
Avery.
Avery who?
Avery merry Christmas to you!

Knock, knock.
Who's there?
Yule.
Yule who?
Yule never know!

Knock, knock.
Who's there?
Snow.
Snow who?
Snow business of yours!

Knock, knock.
Who's there?
Icy.
Icy who?
Icy you in there! Open the door!

Knock, knock.
Who's there?
Abby.
Abby who?
Abby birthday to you!

Knock, knock.
Who's there?
Irish.
Irish who?
Irish you a Merry Christmas!

Knock, knock.
Who's there?
Sandy.
Sandy who?
Sandy Claus!

Knock, knock.
Who's there?
Howl.
Howl who?
Howl you be dressing up for Halloween this year?

Knock, knock.
Who's there?
Dexter.
Dexter who?
Dexter halls with boughs of holly!

Knock, knock.
Who's there?
Phillip.
Phillip who?
Phillip my bag with Halloween candy!

Knock, knock.
Who's there?
Oakham.
Oakham who?
Oakham all ye faithful!

Knock, knock.
Who's there?
Wanda.
Wanda who?
Wanda wish you a happy birthday!

Knock, knock.
Who's there?
Hannah.
Hannah who?
Hannah partridge in a pear tree.

Knock, knock.
Who's there?
Value.
Value who?
Value be my Valentine?

Knock, knock.
Who's there?
Snow.
Snow who?
Snow use, I forgot my name!

Knock, knock.
Who's there?
Mary and Abby.
Mary and Abby who?
Mary Christmas and Abby New Year!

Knock, knock.
Who's there?
Boo.
Boo who?
Don't cry—it's just a knock-knock joke.

4

Food Jokes

Knock, knock.
Who's there?
Honeydew.
Honeydew who?
Honeydew you want to hear a knock knock joke?

Knock, knock.
Who's there?
Orange.
Orange who?
Orange you going to let me in?

Knock, knock.
Who's there?
Doughnut.
Doughnut who?
Doughnut ask, it's a secret!

Knock, knock.
Who's there?
Lettuce.
Lettuce who?
Lettuce in, it's cold out here!

Knock, knock.
Who's there?
Beets.
Beets who?
Beets me!

Knock, knock.
Who's there?
Kiwi.
Kiwi who?
Kiwi go to the store?

Knock, knock.
Who's there?
Cash.
Cash who?
I knew you were a nut!

Knock, knock.
Who's there?
Ice cream.
Ice cream who?
Ice cream if you don't let me in!

Knock, knock.
Who's there?
Turnip.
Turnip who?
Turnip the volume, it's too quiet.

Knock, knock.
Who's there?
Ketchup.
Ketchup who?
Ketchup with you soon!

Knock, knock.
Who's there?
Beef.
Beef who?
Beef-or I get cold, you'd better let me in!

Knock, knock.
Who's there?
Cook.
Cook who?
Hey! Who you calling cuckoo?

Knock, knock.
Who's there?
Bean.
Bean who?
Bean fishing lately?

Knock, knock.
Who's there?
Figs.
Figs who?
Figs the doorbell, it's broken!

Knock, knock.
Who's there?
Aida.
Aida who?
**Aida sandwich for lunch today.
Do you want one?**

Knock, knock.
Who's there?
Bean.
Bean who?
Bean a while since I saw you last!

Knock, knock.
Who's there?
Broccoli.
Broccoli who?
Broccoli doesn't have a last name, silly!

Knock, knock.
Who's there?
Water.
Water who?
Water way to answer the door!

Knock, knock.
Who's there?
Omelet.
Omelet who?
Omelet smarter than I look.

Knock, knock.
Who's there?
You be.
You be who?
You be a pal and bring me a cookie!

Knock, knock.
Who's there?
Orange juice.
Orange juice who?
Orange juice going to invite me in?

Knock, knock.
Who's there?
Butter.
Butter who?
It's butter if you don't know!

Knock, knock.
Who's there?
Doughnut.
Doughnut who?
Doughnut be afraid, it's just me!

Knock, knock.
Who's there?
Peas.
Peas who?
Peas open the door for me!

Knock, knock.
Who's there?
Water.
Water who?
Water you doing?

Knock, knock.
Who's there?
Cereal.
Cereal who?
Cereal pleasure to meet you!

Knock, knock.
Who's there?
Banana.
Banana who?
Knock, knock.
Who's there?
Banana.
Banana who?
Knock, knock.
Who's there?
Orange.
Orange who?
Orange you glad I didn't say banana?

5

Animal Jokes

Knock, knock.
Who's there?
Rhino.
Rhino who?
Rhino every knock knock joke there is!

Knock, knock.
Who's there?
Honeybee.
Honeybee who?
Honeybee a dear and open the door.

Knock, knock.
Who's there?
Alpaca.
Alpaca who?
Alpaca the trunk, you pack the suitcase.

Knock, knock.
Who's there?
A herd.
A herd who?
A herd you were home, so I came over!

Knock, knock.
Who's there?
Gorilla.
Gorilla who?
Gorilla me a steak, I'm hungry!

Dog: Tell me a joke.
Boy: You don't understand human jokes.
Dog: Why? Because humans are so much smarter than dogs?

Boy: Knock, knock.
Dog: Hold on! There's someone at the door! Be right back to hear the joke after I go see who's there!

Knock, knock.
Who's there?
Cowsgo.
Cowsgo who?
No, they don't. Cowsgo moo!

Knock, knock.
Who's there?
Beaver.
Beaver who?
Beaver-y quiet and no one will hear us!

Knock, knock.
Who's there?
Toucan.
Toucan who?
Toucan play that game!

Knock, knock.
Who's there?
Wood ant.
Wood ant who?
Don't be afraid. I wood ant hurt a fly!

Knock, knock.
Who's there?
Bat.
Bat who?
Bat you'll never guess!

Knock, knock.
Who's there?
Kanga.
Kanga who?
No, kanga roo!

Knock, knock.
Who's there?
Howl.
Howl who?
Howl you know if you don't open the door?

Knock, knock.
Who's there?
Giraffe.
Giraffe who?
Giraffe anything to eat, I'm starving!

Knock, knock.
Who's there?
Aurora
Aurora who?
Aurora just came from a polar bear!

Knock, knock.
Who's there?
Meow.
Meow who?
Take meow to the ball game!

Knock, knock.
Who's there?
Owls.
Owls who?
That's right, owls whooooooooo!

Knock, knock.
Who's there?
Lion.
Lion who?
Lion on your doorstep, open up!

Knock, knock.
Who's there?
Amos.
Amos who?
Amos-quito!

Knock, knock.
Who's there?
Anudder.
Anudder who?
Anudder mosquito!

Knock, knock.
Who's there?
Goat.
Goat who?
Goat to the door and find out!

Knock, knock.
Who's there?
Crab.
Crab who?
Crab me a snack, please!

Knock, knock.
Who's there?
Interrupting cow.
Interrupting c—
Mooooo!

Knock, knock.
Who's there?
Cook.
Cook who?
Stop making bird noises and open the door!

Knock, knock.
Who's there?
Who.
Who who?
Are you an owl?

Knock, knock.
Who's there?
Beehive.
Beehive who?
Beehive yourself!

Knock, knock.
Who's there?
Iguana.
Iguana who?
Iguana tell you another knock knock joke!

Knock, knock.
Who's there?
Beehive.
Beehive who?
Beehive yourself.

Knock, knock.
Who's there?
Banana.
Banana who?
Aren't you glad I didn't say knock knock joke?

6

Object
Jokes

Knock, knock
Who's there?
Radio.
Radio who?
Radio not, here I come!

Knock, knock.
Who's there?
Canoe.
Canoe who?
Canoe come over and play?

Knock, knock.
Who's there?
Wooden shoe.
Wooden shoe who?
Wooden shoe like to know?

Knock, knock.
Who's there?
I eat mop.
I eat mop who?
You do what??

Knock, knock.
Who's there?
Dishes.
Dishes who?
Dishes me, who are you?

Knock, knock.
Who's there?
Cargo.
Cargo who?
Cargo "beep, beep, vroom, vroom!"

Knock, knock.
Who's there?
Juicy.
Juicy who?
Juicy my set of keys?

Knock, knock.
Who's there?
Needle.
Needle who?
Needle little money for the movies!

Knock, knock.
Who's there?
One shoe.
One shoe who?
One shoe play with me?

Knock, knock.
Who's there?
A broken pencil.
A broken pencil who?
Never mind. It's pointless!

Knock, knock.
Who's there?
Dishes.
Dishes who?
Dishes the FBI, open up!

Knock, knock.
Who's there?
Fiddle.
Fiddle who?
Fiddle make you happy, I'll tell you!

Knock, knock.
Who's there?
Stopwatch.
Stopwatch who?
Stopwatch you're doing right this minute!

Knock, knock.
Who's there?
Razor.
Razor who?
Razor hands in the air like you just don't care!

Knock, knock.
Who's there?
Train.
Train who?
Someone needs to train ya to open the door!

Knock, knock.
Who's there?
Dishes.
Dishes who?
Dishes a nice place!

Knock, knock.
Who's there?
Wooden shoe.
Wooden shoe who?
Wooden shoe like to hear another joke?

Knock, knock.
Who's there?
Knock.
Knock who?
Knock Knock!
Who's there?
Knock.
Knock who?
Knock Knock!
Who's there?
Knock.
Knock who?
Knock Knock!
Who's there?
Knock.
Knock who?
Knock Knock!
. . . . Ok, well come on in then.

Knock, knock.
Who's there?
Yah!
Yah who?
Did I just hear a cowboy in there?

Knock, knock.
Who's there?
Mustache.
Mustache who?
Please let me in. I mustache you a question!

Knock, knock.
Who's there?
Weevil.
Weevil who?
Weevil only be staying a minute.

Knock, knock.
Who's there?
Says.
Says who?
Says me, that's who!

Knock, knock.
Who's there?
Ear.
Ear who?
Ear you are! I've been looking for you!

Knock, knock.
Who's there?
Sing.
Sing who?
Whoooooo!

Knock, knock.
It's open!

Knock, knock.
Who's there?
Bingo.
Bingo who?
Bingo'ng to come see you for ages?

Knock, knock.
Who's there?
Ammonia.
Ammonia who?
Ammonia little kid!

Knock, knock.
Who's there?
I am.
I am who?
**You mean you don't remember
who you are?**

Knock, knock.
Who's there?
Ears.
Ears who?
**Ears some more knock knock
jokes for you!**

Knock, knock.
Who's there?
Bless.
Bless who?
I didn't sneeze!

Knock, knock.
Who's there?
Dots.
Dots who?
Dots for me to know and you to find out!

Knock, knock.
Who's there?
Winner.
Winner who?
Winner you going to let me in?

Knock, knock.
Who's there?
Scold.
Scold who?
Scold outside!

Knock, knock.
Who's there?
Hebrews.
Hebrews who?
Hebrews some good coffee.

Will you remember me in a minute?
Yes.
Will you remember me in an hour?
Yes.
Will you remember me in a day?
Yes.
Will you remember me in a week?
Yes.
Will you remember me forever?
Yes.
Knock, knock.
Who's there?
You didn't remember me!

Knock, knock.
Who's there?
You know.
You know who?
Ah. It's You-know-who!

Knock, knock.
Who's there?
Leaf.
Leaf who?
Leaf me alone!

Knock, knock.
Who's there?
Diploma.
Diploma who?
Diploma is here to fix the sink.

Knock, knock.
Who's there?
Repeat.
Repeat who?
Who, who, who, who, who.
How long do I have to do this?

Knock, knock.
Who's there?
Hoover.
Hoover who?
Hoover you expecting?

Knock, knock.
Who's there?
Yukon.
Yukon who?
Yukon say that again!

Knock, knock.
Who's there?
Nobel.
Nobel who?
No bell, that's why I knocked!

Knock, knock.
Who's there?
Disguise.
Disguise who?
Disguise your best friend!

Knock, knock.
Who's there?
Freeze
Freeze Who?
Freeze a Jolly Good Fellow!
Freeze a Jolly Good Fellow!
Freeze a Jolly Good Fellow!
Which nobody can deny!

Knock, knock.
Who's there?
Usher.
Usher who?
Usher wish you would let me in!

Knock, knock.
Who's there?
Churchill.
Churchill who?
Churchill be held on Sunday!

Knock, knock.
Who's there?
Noise.
Noise who?
Noise to see you! How have you been?

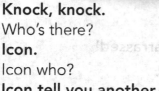

Knock, knock.
Who's there?
Icon.
Icon who?
Icon tell you another knock knock joke if you want!

Knock, knock.
Who's there?
Argue.
Argue who?
Argue going to let me in?

Knock, knock.
Who's there?
Summertime.
Summertime who?
Summertime you can be a big pest!

Knock, knock.
Who's there?
Bashful.
Bashful who?
I can't say, I'm too embarrassed!

Knock, knock.
Who's there?
Passion.
Passion who?
Passion through and thought I'd come say hello!

Knock, knock.
Who's there?
Woo.
Woo who?
Don't get so excited, it's just a joke!

Knock, knock.
Who's there?
Knee.
Knee who?
Knee-d you ask?

Knock, knock.
Who's there?
Dozen.
Dozen who?
Dozen anybody want to let me in?

Knock, knock.
Who's there?
A little old lady.
A little old lady who?
I didn't know you could yodel!

Knock, knock.
Who's there?
Hatch.
Hatch who?
God bless you!

Knock, knock.
Who's there?
Hacienda.
Hacienda who?
Hacienda the joke!

Knock, knock.
Who's there?
Issue.
Issue who?
Issue blind? It's me!

Knock, knock.
Who's there?
Tank.
Tank who?
You're welcome!

Knock, knock.
Who's there?
Ratio.
Ratio who?
Ratio to the end of the street!

Knock, knock.
Who's there?
Hominy.
Hominy who?
Hominy times are we going to have to go through this?

Knock, knock.
Who's there?
Police.
Police who?
Police hurry up, it's chilly outside!

Knock, knock.
Who's there?
Knock, knock.
Who's there?
You're supposed to say "knock knock who!"

Knock, knock.
Who's there?
Impatient pirate.
Impatient p—
ARRRRRRRRRR!

Knock, knock.
Who's there?
Opportunity.
Opportunity who?
Opportunity doesn't knock twice!

Knock, knock.
Who's there?
Zany.
Zany who?
Zany body home?

Knock, knock.
Who's there?
Waddle.
Waddle who?
Waddle you give me if I go away?

Knock, knock.
Who's there?
Handsome.
Handsome who?
Handsome money through the keyhole and I'll tell you!

Knock, knock.
Who's there?
Champ.
Champ who?
Champ poo your hair—it's dirty!

Knock, knock.
Who's there?
Tiss.
Tiss who?
Tiss who is good for blowing your nose!

Knock, knock.
Who's there?
Spell.
Spell who?
W-H-O

Knock, knock.
Who's there?
Ya.
Ya who?
Wow. You sure are excited to see me!

Knock, knock.
Who's there?
A little boy.
A little boy who?
A little boy who can't reach the doorbell!

Knock, knock
Who's there?
Voodoo.
Voodoo who?
Voodoo you think you are!

Knock, knock.
Who's there?
Doorbell repairman!
Doorbell repairman who?
Ding dong! My work here is done.

8

Bonus Jokes and Riddles

What happens to a frog's car when it breaks down?
It gets toad away.

What did the duck say when he bought lipstick?
"Put it on my bill."

Why was 6 afraid of 7?
Because 7, 8, 9.

What musical instrument is found in the bathroom?
A tuba toothpaste.

What do you call cheese that's not yours?

Nacho cheese!

What do elves learn in school?
The elf-abet.

Why did the boy bring a ladder to school?
He wanted to go to high school.

Where do pencils go for vacation?
Pencil-vania.

Why did the girl smear peanut butter on the road?
To go with the traffic jam!

Why do bananas have to put on sunscreen before they go to the beach?
Because they might peel.

How do you make a tissue dance?
You put a little boogie in it.

Which flower talks the most?
Tulips, of course, because they have two lips!

**A man arrived in a small town on Friday.
He stayed for two days and left on Friday.
How is this possible?**
His horse's name is Friday!

What did 0 say to 8?
Nice belt!

What did the mushroom say to the fungus?
You're a fun guy [fungi].

Why couldn't the pony sing himself a lullaby?
He was a little hoarse.

What do you get if you cross a parrot with a shark?
A bird that will talk your ear off.

What do you get when you cross a ghost and a cat?
A scaredy cat!

What do you get when you cross a fish and drumsticks?
Fish sticks.

What do you get when you cross a tiger and a blizzard?
Frostbite!

What do you get when you cross a caterpillar and a parrot?

A walkie-talkie!

What do you get when you cross a fish with an elephant?
Swimming trunks.

What do you get when you cross a piece of paper and scissors?
Confetti.

What do you get when you cross a cow and a lawnmower?
A lawn-moo-er.

What do you get when you cross a cow with a trampoline?
A milkshake!

What do you call a cat crossed with a fish?
Catfish.

What do you get
when you cross a
frog with a rabbit?

A bunny ribbit.

What do you get if you cross a fridge and a stereo?
Cool music!

What do you get if you cross a kangaroo and a snake?
A jump rope!

What do you get when you cross a karate expert with a pig?
A pork chop.

What do you get when you cross a chicken and a chihuahua?
Pooched eggs.

What do you get when you cross a lemon and a cat?
A sourpuss.

What do you call a race car that can't race?
A car.

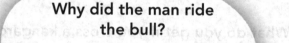

Why did the man ride the bull?

Because it was too heavy to carry.

What does lightning wear under their pants?
Thunderwear.

Why did the boy tiptoe in front of the medicine cabinet?
He didn't want to wake the sleeping pills.

What do you call a deer with no eyes?
No eye deer (no idea)

What do you call a cow that just had a baby?
De-calf-inated.

What do you call cows that are laying down?
Ground beef.

Why did the fastest cat in school get suspended?
Cuz he was a cheetah.

What does a piece of toast wear to bed?
His pa-JAM-as.

What do you call a dinosaur that does not take a bath?
A Stink-o-Saurus.

Why do fish live in salt water?
Because pepper makes them sneeze!

Why did the orange lose the race?
Because he ran out of juice.

Two muffins in an oven.
One says, "Sure is hot in here!"
The other one says, "Holy smokes! A talking muffin!"

What's orange and sounds like a parrot?
A carrot.

**What do you call a boomerang
that does not come back?**
A stick!

**What do you get when you cross
Godzilla and a parrot?**
I don't know, but if he asks for a
cracker, give it to him!

**What do you get if you cross a
kangaroo and an elephant?**
Big holes all over Australia!

What do you get if you cross a cat with an elephant?
A flat cat.

What do you get if you cross a football player with a pay phone?
A wide receiver.

What do you get when you cross a hamburger with a computer?
A big mac!

What do you get when you cross a fly, a car, and a dog?

A flying carpet.

What do you get when you cross an elephant with a witch?
I don't know but she will need a very large broom!

What do you get when you cross a Border Collie and a daisy?
Cauliflower!

What kind of bagel can fly?
A plain bagel.

Why did the opera singer go sailing?
Because she wanted to hit the high C's.

How does the ocean say hello?
It waves.

How do barbers speed up their jobs?
They make short cuts.

What did Tennessee?
The same thing Arkansas.

What do you call a story about a broken pencil?
Pointless.

How do you serve a smart hamburger?
On an honor roll.

Where do cars get the most flat tires?
At forks in the road.

What do you call a blind dinosaur?
A Do-you-think-he-saur-us.

How many books can you put into an empty backpack?
One—after that it isn't empty.

What goes up but never comes down?
Your age.

How many months have 28 days?
All of them.

Which weighs more, a ton of feathers or a ton of bricks?
Neither—they both weigh a ton.

How many letters are in The Alphabet?

There are 11 letters in The Alphabet.

David's father has three sons: Snap, Crackle, and ___?
David.

What has a head and tail, is brown, and has no legs?
A penny.

What is white, has a horn, and gives milk?
A milk truck.

What kind of nut always seems to have a cold?
Cashews.

Waiter, will my pizza be long?
No sir, it will be round.

What is black, white, green, and bumpy?
A pickle wearing a tuxedo.

What do you call candy that's been stolen?
Hot chocolate.

How do you make a walnut laugh?
Crack it up.

How do you make a milk shake?
Give it a good scare.

What is a pretzel's favorite dance?
The twist.

What do you get when you cross a porcupine and a turtle?
A slowpoke.

What do you get when you cross a potato with an elephant?
Mashed potatoes!

What do you get when you cross a mouse with a squid?
An eektopus!

Why do ducks have flat feet?
To stamp out forest fires.

Where does the president keep his armies?
Up his sleevies.

What did one eye say to the other eye?
Don't look now but something between us smells.

A boy asks his father, "Dad, are bugs good to eat?"

"That's disgusting—don't talk about things like that over dinner," the dad replies.

After dinner the father asks, "Now, son, what did you want to ask me?"

"Oh, nothing," the boy says. "There was a bug in your soup, but now it's gone."

A dad and his son were riding their bikes and crashed. Two ambulances came and took them to different hospitals. The man's son was in the operating room and the doctor said, "I can't operate on you. You're my son."

How is that possible?

The doctor is his mom!

What goes up when rain comes down?
An umbrella!

What is the longest word in the dictionary?
Smiles, because there is a mile between the s's.

If I drink, I die.
If I eat, I am fine.
What am I?

A fire!

Throw away the outside and cook the inside, then eat the outside and throw away the inside. What is it?
Corn on the cob, because you throw away the husk, cook and eat the kernels, and throw away the cob.

What has a foot but no legs?
A snail.

Poor people have it. Rich people need it. If you eat it you die. What is it?
Nothing.

What comes down but never goes up?
Rain.

Mr. Blue lives in the blue house, Mr. Pink lives in the pink house, and Mr. Brown lives in the brown house. Who lives in the white house?
The president!

They come out at night without being called, and are lost in the day without being stolen. What are they?
Stars.

How do you make the number one disappear?
Add the letter G and it's "GONE"

What goes up but never comes down?
Your age!

What starts with the letter "t", is filled with "t", and ends in "t"?
A teapot!

What is so delicate that saying its name breaks it?
Silence.

You walk into a room with a match, a kerosene lamp, a candle, and a fireplace. Which do you light first?

The match.

A man was driving his truck. His lights were not on. The moon was not out. Up ahead, a woman was crossing the street. How did he see her?
It was a bright and sunny day!

Lots of Jokes for Kids

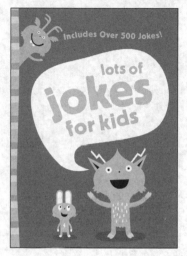

Q: What do you get when you cross a parrot and a centipede?

A: A walkie-talkie!

Q: What kind of light did Noah install on the ark?

A: Floodlights

Introducing a collection of jokes that's hilarious, clean, and kid-friendly and includes everything from knock-knock jokes, to Q&A jokes, tongue twisters, and a whole lot more. *Lots of Jokes for Kids* is certain to have every kid you know laughing out loud, snorting riotously, and generally gasping for air.

Available in stores and online!

Super, Epic, Mega Joke Book for Kids

Whee Winn

The Super, Epic, Mega, Joke Book is just the thing for comedians and joke-lovers, young and old! Kid-friendly and fun, this collection of hundreds of jokes, riddles, tongue twisters, and more will keep everyone giggling for hours.

So, what's the funniest joke you'll find in this book?

Knock, knock.

Who's there?

Lena.

Lena who?

Lena little closer and I'll tell you!